For my children, for my nephews, for my nieces: being different is the thing you will dislike about yourselves, but one day you will hear my old words ringing in your ears: 'why be like everyone else, when you can be like you?' N.H.

For everyone out there who feels a little bit different E.B.

HODDER CHILDREN'S BOOKS

First published in Great Britain in 2021
by Hodder and Stoughton

Text © Nadiya Hussain, 2021
Illustrations © Ella Bailey, 2021

A CIP catalogue record of this book
is available from the British Library.

HB ISBN: 978 1 444 95746 4
PB ISBN: 978 1 444 95747 1

10 9 8 7 6 5 4 3 2 1

Printed and bound in China.

Hodder Children's Books
An imprint of
Hachette Children's Group
Part of Hodder and Stoughton
Carmelite House
50 Victoria Embankment
London, EC4Y 0DZ

An Hachette UK Company
www.hachette.co.uk

www.hachettechildrens.co.uk

Spreading my Wings

Written by
Nadiya Hussain

Illustrated by
Ella Bailey

Hodder
Children's
Books

I am a boy, and this is Rayf, my bird.
He sits on my shoulder.
I am brown . . .

He is yellow and blue with speckles on his neck.
Rayf is my friend.

I talk and laugh and whisper.

He tweets and cheeps and sings.

I like to eat tomatoes
and ice cream.

He loves seeds: big ones that
he cracks, and little ones he can
gulp right down.

Rayf and I have been to lots of places together:
to the supermarket,

to Granny's house

and even to the top of a mountain.

But we have never been to holiday club.
This is our first day.

I am ready. Shoes on, shirt straight.
Rayf is ready. Feathers out, tail straight.

There are boys and girls
everywhere.

Some are painting, some stringing beads.
Some are squashing play dough and others are running around.

They are all busy, but one thing is the same:
none of them has a budgie on their shoulder.

I look up at Rayf, standing proudly with his little feathery chest puffed out. **I feel worried.**

I think:
maybe I should be like
everyone else.
Maybe I shouldn't have
a budgie.

Rayf fluffs up his wings and tries to take off. I hold him down, my hand across his soft back.

I whisper, "You can't fly. Not here."

Rayf looks at me with sad eyes.
Then he hops into my coat pocket and I start to feel
a tiny bit less worried.

As long as Rayf doesn't fly or sing, I will be okay.
No one will know that I am different.

All morning, I play with the other children.
We run, paint, splash and laugh.

Sometimes I think of Rayf, curled up in my pocket and I feel sad.
But then I squash the sad feeling down.

After lunch we put on our coats to go outside.

I can't let Rayf fly. I can't let everyone see that I'm different.

In the garden we all kneel in the grass,
and feel the soft earth between our fingers.

I am excited. I pick up the packet
of carrot seeds and **Shake it** hard.

Seeds fly everywhere!
Then I notice something . . .

Rayf is free!

He flies out of my pocket and **gobbles up** some seeds.

Then he lets out the happiest tweet tweet twiddly twee

he soars through the air.

All the other children are quiet.
I feel my face turning red. I didn't want to be different.

Then everyone speaks at once.

"Did you
see him fly?"

"What kind of
a bird is he?"

"He's so
beautiful!"

"He makes a
lovely sound."

I feel a smile creep across my face.
"You like him?"

The children all smile at me.
Then they shout,
"Let's play!"

I am a boy, and this is Rayf, my bird.
Rayf is my friend.
He sits on my shoulder.

I talk and laugh and whisper. He tweets and cheeps and sings. And when we spread our wings, we **fly** and **swoop** and **soar**.

We are **free**.